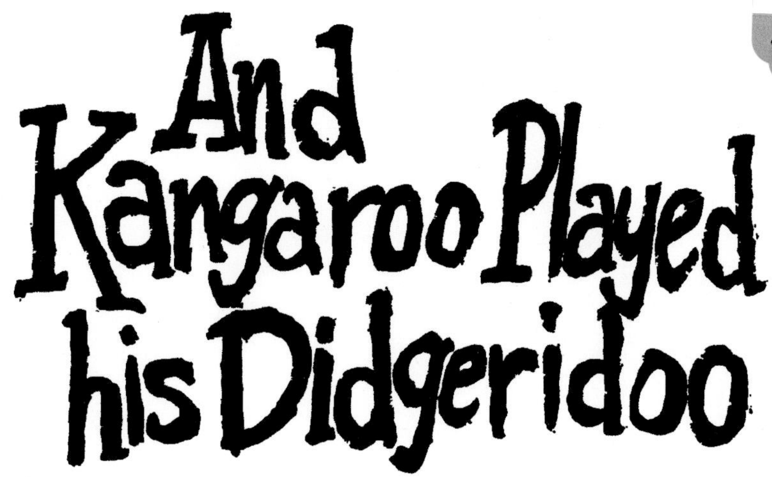

Nigel Gray

illustrated by Glen Singleton

SCHOLASTIC
SYDNEY AUCKLAND NEW YORK TORONTO LONDON

For Eloise and John. NG

*To Janelle and Luke of course,
and to Felicity, Lore, James B. and Michael B. GS*

Gray, Nigel, 1941–.
And kangaroo played his didgeridoo.
ISBN 1 86388 179 4.
1. Children's poetry, Australian. 2. Zoology—Australia—Juvenile poetry.
3. Kangaroos—Juvenile poetry. I. Singleton, Glen, 1959–. II. Title.

A821.3

First published in 1995 by Scholastic Australia Pty Limited
ACN 000 614 577, PO Box 579, Gosford 2250. Also in Sydney, Brisbane,
Melbourne, Adelaide and Perth.

Reprinted in 1996 (twice).

Typeset in 17 pt Oxford.

Printed in Hong Kong.

9 8 7 6 5 4 3 6 7 8 9 / 9

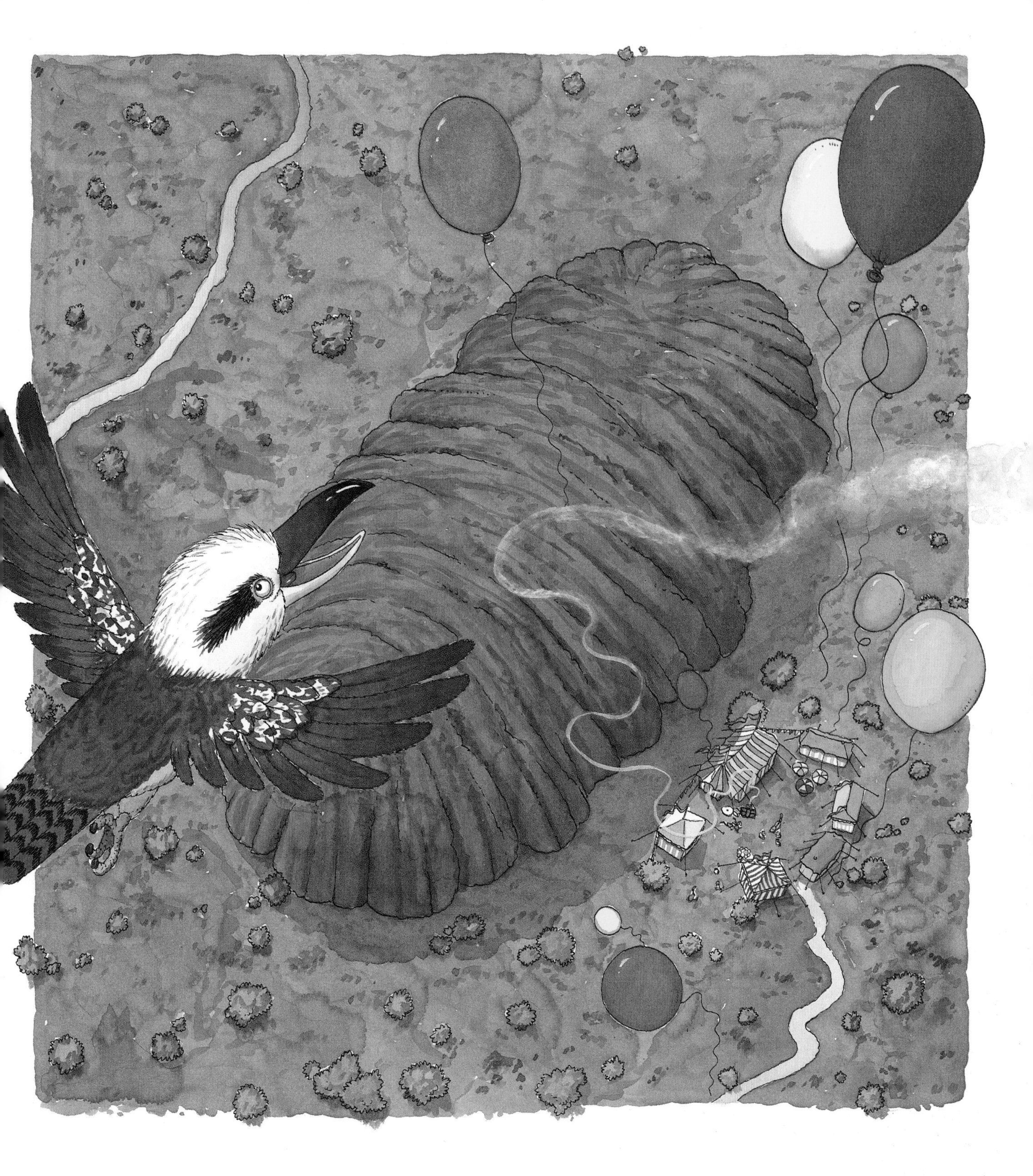

You should have come to the Great Aussie Do,
The guest list read like an Aussie *Who's Who*,
And Kangaroo played his didgeridoo.

They came from all over to Uluru,
Death Adder crawled and Bowerbird flew,

And Kangaroo played his didgeridoo.

SYDNEY
ULURU
BRISBANE

Wallaby travelled from far Kakadu
With Eagle, Echidna and proud Emu,
And Kangaroo played his didgeridoo.

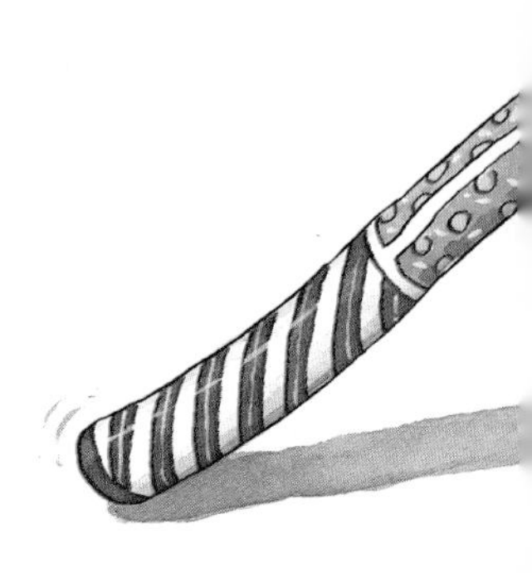

Some made the journey in an old canoe,
Shark was the captain, and Dolphin the crew,

And Kangaroo played his didgeridoo.

Kingfisher came wearing green and blue,
Possum looked pretty in her pink tutu,
And Kangaroo played his didgeridoo.

Bandicoot, as always, looked well-to-do,
But best dressed of all was White Cockatoo,
And Kangaroo played his didgeridoo.

In the crush, Frilled Lizard lost a shoe,
While Goanna's wig was knocked all askew,

And Kangaroo played his didgeridoo.

Budgie and Parrot played peek-a-boo,
Gecko was sporting a stick-on tattoo,
And Kangaroo played his didgeridoo.

Said Numbat to Wombat, 'How do you do?'
Said Wombat, 'No worries! How about you?'
And Kangaroo played his didgeridoo.

Dingo served fruit juice with young Wallaroo,
Booby was cook at the beaut barbecue,

And Kangaroo played his didgeridoo.

Pelican pushed to the front of the queue,
Galah bit off much more than she could chew,

And Kangaroo played his didgeridoo.

Penguin and Platypus planned a rendezvous,
Tree Frog told Turtle he'd always be true,
And Kangaroo played his didgeridoo.

Sweet Jillaroo danced with wild Jackeroo,
Till Koala caused a hullabaloo,
And Kangaroo played his didgeridoo.

Then Thorny Devil had a set to,
With Legless Lizard—oh what a to-do!

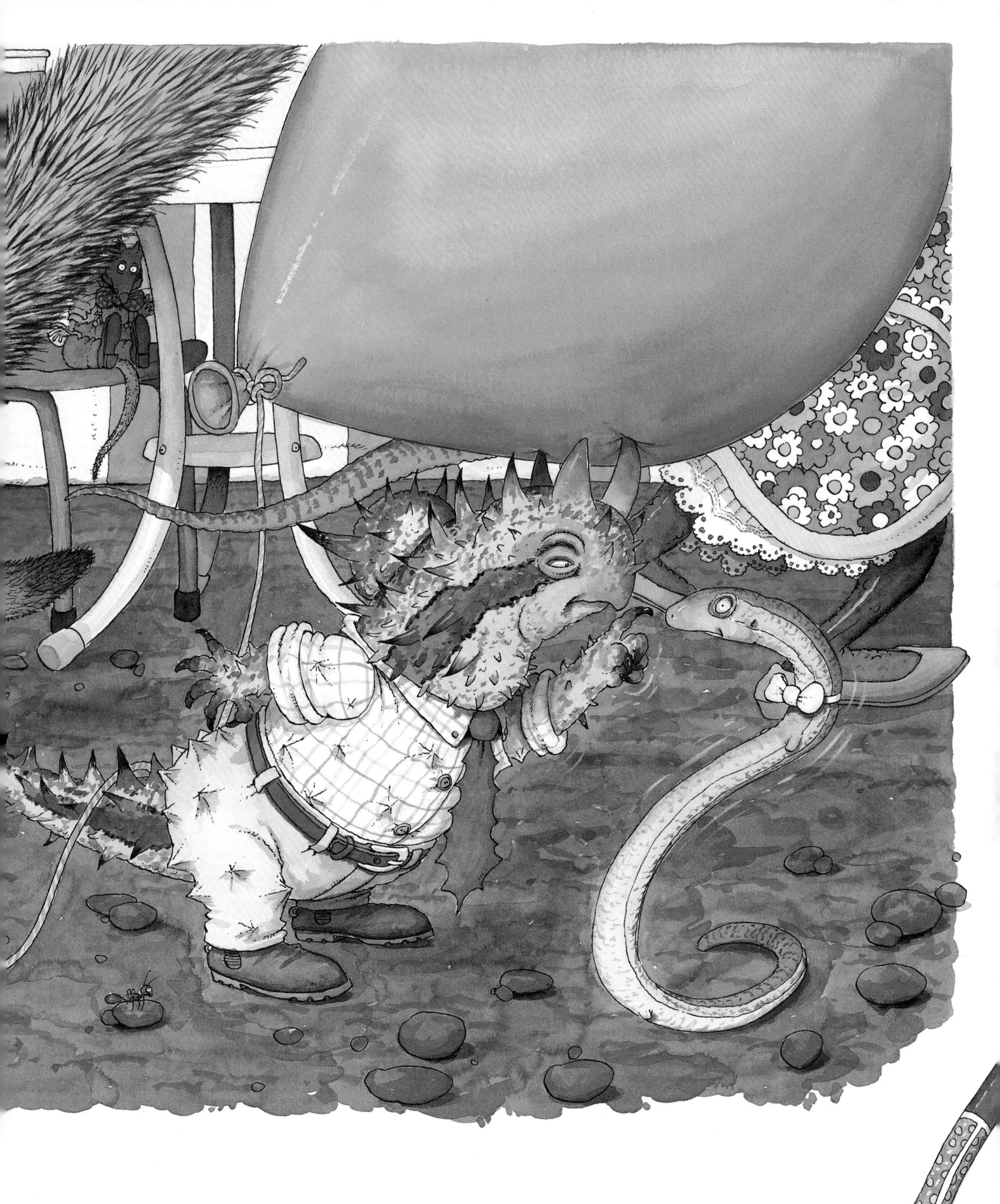

And Kangaroo played his didgeridoo.

Old Crocodile cried, ‘Boo-hoo, boo-hoo’,
Just crocodile tears as I guess you knew,

And Kangaroo played his didgeridoo.

Rat played a rhythm with bits of bamboo,
Quokka let rip on his brand new kazoo,
And Kangaroo played his didgeridoo.

Kookaburra laughed and Trumpet Fish blew,
And Owl joined in with, 'Tu-whit' and 'tu-whoo',
And Kangaroo played his didgeridoo.

The party continued the whole night through,
Bat had a ball, till the night birds' curfew,

And Kangaroo played his didgeridoo.

The food was all eaten by half past two,
When the sun came up, Bilby made a brew,

And Kangaroo played his didgeridoo.

We danced and we pranced and we Skipped To My Lou,
We sang and we laughed with old friends and new,
And Kangaroo played his didgeridoo,
At the once-in-a-lifetime, Great Aussie Do.